Bad New

Nancy, Bess, and George were almost to the house when they heard the front door open. "They're coming out," Nancy whispered. "Hide!"

The girls ducked behind a row of bushes.

"I'll speak to Mr. Drew right away," they heard Hannah say. "I'm sure he'll understand."

"Good," Mrs. Garfield replied. "Then I'll see you a week from Friday."

A short while later the girls heard Hannah's car drive away.

"This is terrible." Nancy sniffled. "I wish we'd never come here."

"Come on, let's go," Bess whispered. The girls stood up and saw that the big, black gate was slowly swinging shut.

"Hurry!" George cried. "Or we'll be trapped!"

The Nancy Drew Notebooks

Available from MINSTREL Books

#20

THE NANCY DREW NOTEBOOKS®

HANNAH'S SECRET

CAROLYN KEENE

Illustrated by Anthony Accardo

A MINSTREL® BOOK

PUBLISHED BY POCKET BOOKS

New York   London   Toronto   Sydney   Tokyo   Singapore

A MINSTREL PAPERBACK *Original*

A Minstrel Book published by
POCKET BOOKS, a division of Simon & Schuster Inc.
1230 Avenue of the Americas, New York, NY 10020

Copyright © 1997 by Simon & Schuster Inc.
Produced by Mega-Books, Inc.

ISBN: 0-671-56864-7

First Minstrel Books printing September 1997

10 9 8 7 6 5 4 3 2 1

NANCY DREW, THE NANCY DREW NOTEBOOKS, A MINSTREL BOOK and colophon are registered trademarks of Simon & Schuster Inc.

Cover art by Aleta Jenks

Printed in the U.S.A.

1

A Delicious Lesson

"**G**uess what, Daddy? I'm helping Hannah make dessert," eight-year-old Nancy Drew said into the phone.

"That's great," Carson Drew said on the other end of the line. Nancy's father was a lawyer. He was on a business trip and was calling from his hotel room in California. "Are you making pudding or pie?" he asked.

Nancy giggled. Pudding Pie was one of her father's favorite nicknames for her. One time she had eaten a huge piece of chocolate-pudding pie with her hands and ended up with chocolate all over her face. There was a picture of it in the family photo album.

"Neither," Nancy said. "We're making apple cake. Hannah's teaching me the recipe."

"Just make sure you eat your dinner before your dessert," Mr. Drew said. "And try not to cause too much trouble for Hannah, all right? I'll see you both Friday night."

"Okay, Daddy." Nancy said goodbye and hung up. She skipped across the kitchen, pausing just long enough to give her puppy, Chocolate Chip, a pat on the head.

"Let's get cooking," Hannah Gruen said to Nancy. She was the family's housekeeper. "But wash your hands first. I don't want any dog fur in our cake."

"Ick!" Nancy loved Chip, but she didn't think her Labrador retriever's brown fur would taste very good.

Nancy quickly washed her hands and held them up for Hannah to see. "All clean."

2

Then she dipped her finger into the mixing bowl on the counter.

Hannah pushed Nancy's hand away. "Be careful," she said with a smile. "When I was a little girl, I once ate half a bowl of cake batter. I had a stomachache for three days!"

Nancy giggled and looked at Hannah's gentle face. It was hard to imagine her as a little girl.

"Why didn't your mother stop you from eating so much?" she asked.

"She tried," Hannah said. "But I sneaked in and gobbled it up when she wasn't looking."

Nancy laughed again. "I didn't know you were such a bad little girl."

"I wasn't *that* bad," Hannah said with a twinkle in her eye. "Didn't a certain little girl spill my favorite houseplant all over the living room floor last week?"

Nancy glanced over at her puppy. "I forgot about that," she said, giving Hannah a sweet smile. Chip had bumped into the plant when she and Nancy were playing in the den.

"Just remember," Hannah said, "no more fetch in the house." She pushed her hair off her forehead and smiled at Nancy. "The cake batter is just about ready. All we need to add are the apples and nuts."

Hannah had already cut up three apples. Nancy picked up the bowl and dumped the pieces into the batter. As Nancy stirred, Hannah added some chopped walnuts.

"How did you learn to be such a good cook, Hannah?" Nancy asked.

"I learned most of my recipes from my grandmother when I was growing up. She's also the one who taught me how to make a pretty garden."

"Maybe after you show me how to cook, you can teach me all about flowers," Nancy suggested.

"Maybe." Hannah winked. "Though, as I recall, the last time I tried to get you to help with the gardening, all you wanted to do was make mud pies."

Nancy rolled her eyes. "Hannah, I was only four years old then!"

"I'm just teasing," Hannah said, giving Nancy a fond look. "Before I know it, you'll be all grown up and I'll be out of a job."

"Never," Nancy said. "You'll still need to stay here and take care of Daddy. He'll *never* grow up!"

Hannah and Nancy laughed. "I think the batter is just about ready," Hannah said, shaking some cinnamon into the bowl. "Do you want to put it into the pan?"

Nancy nodded eagerly as Hannah poured half the batter from the mixing bowl into a measuring cup. "It will be easier for you to pour this way," Hannah said.

Nancy carefully poured all the batter into a cake pan—just the way Hannah showed her.

"Nice job," Hannah said, sliding the

pan into the oven. "You'll be able to cook all by yourself in no time."

"It won't be *that* soon," Nancy said. "I'm not allowed to use the oven until I'm ten, remember?"

"That's right." Hannah tousled Nancy's reddish blond hair. Then she looked at the oven timer. "I'm not sure how long the cake is supposed to bake. Would you get me my recipe book so I can look it up?"

"You mean your *secret* recipe book?" Nancy asked.

Hannah kept all of her best recipes in a pretty handmade book with roses on the cover. She didn't like anyone to look inside it.

Nancy understood how Hannah felt because she had a special book, too. Nancy liked to solve mysteries, and her father had given her a shiny blue notebook. In it she wrote down her clues and suspects.

"Don't worry," she said, looking for

Hannah's cookbook on the shelf above the counter. "I won't peek."

Nancy wobbled high on her tiptoes and grabbed the recipe book. But she lost her balance. The book slipped right out of her hand—and came flying straight toward her head!

2

A Strange Note

Nancy jumped out of the way just in time. The recipe book bounced off the counter and fell to the floor with a thump. A few pieces of paper came fluttering out.

"Are you all right?" Hannah cried, hurrying over.

Nancy nodded. She helped Hannah pick up the papers. Most of them were recipes in Hannah's handwriting. Except the last one. It was a note that said:

Meeting—12 Riverview Lane.
Sat. 10—wear suit.

I wonder why Hannah has to wear a suit? Nancy thought. Her meeting must be someplace fancy.

"You're not peeking at any of those recipes, are you?" Hannah asked.

Nancy shook her head and quickly handed Hannah the cards.

Hannah stuck them back in the book. Then she turned to an inside page. "Here it is," she said. "The cake should bake for forty minutes."

As Hannah and Nancy ate dinner, Nancy could smell the apples and cinnamon baking. When the cake was done, Hannah took it out of the oven. After it had cooled a little, she cut two big slices and put a scoop of vanilla ice cream on top of each one.

"Mmm, that was super yummy, Hannah," Nancy said when she had finished eating. "May I be excused?"

"Not so fast," Hannah said gently. "Aren't you forgetting something?"

Nancy groaned and started taking

the plates from the table. "I hate clearing the dishes."

"Just leave everything in the sink," Hannah said, heading for the stairs. "I'll load the dishwasher later."

Nancy sighed as she brought the dirty dishes from the table to the sink. Chip followed her.

"I wish you could do this for me," Nancy said to her puppy. She smiled at the thought of Chip carrying the plates and forks in her mouth. "Maybe I should train you to load the dishwasher, too."

When the table was clear, Nancy went upstairs, with Chip right behind her. Hannah's door was closed, but Nancy could hear her humming.

Chip raced into Nancy's room and picked up her favorite toy bone from the floor. She brought it to Nancy.

Nancy sat on the floor and took it from Chip's mouth. "Want to play?" she asked.

Chip looked up at Nancy and barked twice.

"I guess that means yes." She glanced at Hannah's door on the other side of the hall. "But be careful, okay?"

Nancy tossed the toy across the room. Chip bounded after it and brought the bone back to her.

"Good dog," Nancy said.

Just then Nancy heard Hannah's bedroom door open. She peeked out into the hall, hoping Hannah wasn't going to scold her for playing fetch in the house. Instead, Hannah picked up the phone and started to dial.

Nancy ducked back out of sight and scratched Chip's tummy to keep her quiet. "We'll finish playing as soon as Hannah goes back in her room," she whispered. Then Nancy heard Hannah talking.

"Hello, Joan? It's Hannah."

Nancy knew that Joan was one of Hannah's good friends. She was the

housekeeper for a family on the other side of town.

"Yes, I'm going on Saturday at ten," Hannah continued. "I'm looking forward to it, though I'm a bit nervous. I hope it goes well."

I wonder what Hannah's doing on Saturday, Nancy thought. She remembered the note that had fallen out of Hannah's secret recipe book.

Then Hannah paused to listen to something Joan was saying. "Yes," Hannah went on, "but I also think she'll make a terrific boss."

"Why would Hannah care if someone's a good boss?" Nancy whispered to Chip. She thought for a minute. "The note said something about a meeting on Saturday morning and wearing a suit."

Nancy gasped. Grown-ups wore suits when they looked for jobs! And Hannah had just told Joan that the person she was seeing on Saturday would make a great boss.

Nancy had a terrible idea about what Hannah's note might mean. She picked up her puppy and hugged her tightly.

"Oh, Chip," she cried, burying her face in the dog's soft brown fur. "Could it be true? Is Hannah going to leave us?"

3

Nosy Brenda

Nancy had to talk to Hannah about what she had heard. She was nervous, but she took a deep breath and walked into the hall. Hannah had finished her call and was in her room again.

Just as Nancy was about to knock on Hannah's door, it opened.

Hannah looked down at Nancy and quickly closed it again. Before she did, Nancy saw papers spread all over her desk.

"Hannah?" Nancy called. "What are you doing?"

Hannah's muffled voice came from the other side of the door. "Just a minute, Nancy."

Nancy frowned. Hannah's keeping a secret, Nancy thought. She didn't like that. "Never mind," Nancy called loudly, and stomped back to her room.

Chip was waiting there with her toy bone in her mouth. "Sorry, Chip, I can't play right now," Nancy said. "Hannah's acting weird, and I think I know why. I'd better start treating this like a real mystery so I can find out for sure."

Nancy went to her desk and found her blue notebook under her backpack. Opening to a fresh page, she wrote: "Hannah's Mysterious Secret."

Under that she wrote, "Does Hannah want another job?" Then she listed her clues:

1. Hannah has a meeting on Saturday.
2. She's wearing a suit to the meeting.
3. She said the person she's

meeting will make a great boss.
4. She doesn't want me in her room.

Nancy read over what she had just written. Then she remembered what Hannah had been talking about earlier that evening. She added one more clue:

5. Hannah may think I don't need her anymore.

"What else could it mean, Chip?" Nancy asked.

The Labrador retriever yawned.

Hannah had been taking care of Nancy ever since she was three years old. Nancy loved her and didn't want Hannah ever to leave.

She wished she could talk to her father about her problem. But it was only Wednesday, and he wouldn't be home until Friday night.

Still, she knew one thing he would say if he were here—not to jump to conclusions. The clues could mean Hannah was leaving, or something totally different. But what?

Nancy needed help. She went to the phone to call her two best friends, Bess Marvin and George Fayne.

The next day Nancy met Bess and George outside Mrs. Reynolds's third-grade classroom.

"Did you find any more clues, Nancy?" Bess asked.

Nancy shook her head. "I can't believe Hannah might be looking for another job," she said.

George put her arm around Nancy. "But it doesn't mean she definitely wants to leave," she said. "My dad had an interview last month, but he likes it where he is, so he decided not to take the job."

"But what if it's a really great job?" Nancy glanced around at the other

kids in the hall. She didn't want anyone to overhear. "Hannah might go
away and I'll never see her again," she
whispered.

"She already has a great job," Bess
said loyally. She pushed her blond
hair out of her eyes. "Don't worry,
Nancy. You'll figure out what's going
on."

Just then their classmate Brenda
Carlton walked up to them. "What are
you guys talking about?" she asked.

Brenda was always trying to find
things to write about for her newspa-
per, the *Carlton News*. All the kids in
their class read it.

"None of your business," Nancy
said. She didn't want anyone else to
know about her mystery—especially
Brenda.

"Everything is my business,"
Brenda said with a smirk. "You're
hiding something, Nancy, and I'm
going to find out what it is!" Brenda's

dark brown hair flipped as she turned and stomped into the classroom.

All day Nancy thought about the mystery every chance she had. She tried to talk about it with Bess and George at lunch, but Brenda sat at their table without being invited.

After school Nancy met Bess and George on the steps outside the building. Brenda was standing nearby. Nancy could tell she was trying to listen to what they were saying.

"We have to talk about the mystery," Nancy said. She looked over at Brenda. "But where *someone* can't follow us."

"Let's go to my house," George said.

Nancy hurried home to get permission. Then she rode to George's house as fast as her bike would take her.

When all three girls were in George's room, Nancy took out her mystery notebook. Bess and George flopped on the bed.

"Let's think about why Hannah might want to leave," Nancy said.

"Maybe she works too hard," Bess suggested.

Hannah did work pretty hard, Nancy thought. She was always cleaning up after Chip or reminding Nancy to do her chores, the way she had last night.

George shook her head. "I bet she just wants more money."

"Maybe," Nancy said, sitting down next to her friends. She grabbed a pillow and sighed. "This is awful."

"It doesn't matter," Bess said quickly. "If Hannah wants to leave, the important thing is to change her mind."

"Maybe if we know what kind of job she's trying to get, we can find a way to talk her out of taking it," Nancy said.

"But how?" George asked.

"I know where her meeting is," Nancy said. "It's at Twelve Riverview

Lane." She had copied Hannah's note in her book that morning when Hannah wasn't looking. "We just have to find it."

George asked her mother if they could go for a ride. Then Nancy, Bess, and George hopped on their bikes.

Riverview Lane was a longer street than Nancy had thought. She and her friends rode past the movie theater, the bowling alley, and lots of stores.

When they got to a toy store, the girls stopped to look at a big teddy bear in the window.

Nancy looked at her reflection in the glass. Then she saw something behind her. She quickly glanced back to make sure it was true. Brenda was hiding in back of a mailbox with her bike!

"Brenda's following us," Nancy said. "We have to lose her."

"Oh no," Bess said. "Do you think she knows what we're doing?"

"Not yet," George said. "Let's split up."

23

"Good idea," Nancy said. "We'll meet by the bowling alley in a few minutes. One, two, three, *go!*"

The three girls sped away as fast as they could. When they got to the corner, Nancy turned left, Bess turned right, and George sped straight ahead. Within minutes the plan had worked. Brenda was gone.

"We did it!" Nancy cried when the three friends met up again.

A few minutes later, Nancy, Bess, and George were standing with their bikes in front of 12 Riverview Lane. It was a large white house with a wall around the yard. A big *G* was on the black iron gate.

"I know who lives here," Bess said. "Mrs. Garfield. She was at my house yesterday. My mom's working on a charity with her. She looks like a mean old crab."

Nancy giggled. "Old Mrs. Crabapple!"

Bess and George laughed, too. But

they all stopped when the front door of the house opened.

"Shhh!" Nancy said, and carefully peeked around the gatepost. She saw a grumpy-looking old woman with short gray hair climb into a car. Then the black gate started to open.

"Don't let Old Crabapple see us spying!" George said.

The three girls quickly wheeled their bikes across the street just as the car came through and drove away.

"She's creepy," Nancy said.

Suddenly, Bess's eyes widened. "Oh no!"

"What?" Nancy and George asked at the same time.

"I know what kind of job Hannah's looking for," Bess said. "Yesterday Old Crabapple told my mom she needs a new housekeeper!"

4

Operation Cleanup

I guess it must be true," Nancy said as the girls biked home. "Old Crabapple needs a housekeeper, and Hannah has an interview with her on Saturday. She's really leaving. Case closed."

George shook her head until her dark curls bounced. "No way," she said. "We can't let Hannah work for a nasty old woman. It would be horrible."

George was right. Nancy had to think of a way to make Hannah want to stay. Hannah's interview wasn't until Saturday. There was still hope.

When Nancy got home, she found Hannah in the kitchen, feeding Chip.

"Dinner should be ready soon," Hannah said.

Nancy scratched Chip behind the ears. "Can I do anything to help?"

"How nice of you to offer," Hannah said, looking pleased. "You could set the table."

"Can we eat in the dining room tonight?" Nancy asked Hannah. She wanted to make their dinner extra special.

"Okay," Hannah said. "We're having hamburgers, so don't forget the ketchup."

Nancy carried the dishes Hannah handed her to the dining room as Chocolate Chip jumped around her feet. Then she opened the wooden cabinet against the wall.

There's lots of fancy stuff in here, Nancy said to herself. She picked up a beautiful plate. I'm going to make the table superspecial. That way Hannah will see that dinner here can be just as nice as at Old Crabapple's fancy house.

Chip put her paws on Nancy's knees. Nancy gently pushed her down. "Don't trip me," she warned. "I don't want to break anything."

She set a crystal glass at each place, admiring the way they made the whole table seem prettier.

"Okay, what else?" Nancy said, going back to the cabinet. "How about these cloth napkins, Chip?"

"Woof," Chip answered.

"I agree." Nancy laughed. "They're perfect."

By the time Hannah came in with the food, the table was ready. Nancy had set shiny silver forks on top of the napkins. The butter was in a crystal dish and the ketchup in a china gravy boat.

Hannah laughed when she saw what Nancy had done. "Are you expecting the President for dinner?"

Nancy shrugged. "I just thought it

would be fun to use these dishes. It looks nice, doesn't it?"

"It's beautiful," Hannah said, setting down the food and taking her seat. "Most of these fancy dishes are very delicate. I'll have to be careful when I hand-wash them."

"Oops," Nancy said, trying to smile. Extra work for Hannah wasn't part of her plan. "I didn't think about that. I'll wash the dishes myself."

"Don't be silly," Hannah said, reaching for the ketchup. "I don't mind."

After dinner Nancy cleared the table without being asked. Then she went upstairs to use the phone.

She called Bess and told her the whole story. "Now I have to think of another nice thing to do for Hannah."

"You could clean your room," Bess suggested.

"That's a good idea," Nancy said. "But what if I cleaned the whole house tomorrow as a surprise?"

"That sounds like a lot of work,"

Bess said doubtfully. "But I'll come over and help."

"Great," Nancy said. "I'll ask George to come, too. I'm going to need all the help I can get!"

The next day Nancy, Bess, and George went to Nancy's house after school. Hannah was upstairs. The girls called hello to her and went into the living room.

Chip was already there, lying next to the couch.

"Where do we start?" Bess asked. She wrinkled her nose. "I hope you don't want us to clean the bathroom."

Nancy looked around. "Let's start in here," she said. "I'll vacuum."

"I'll dust the furniture," Bess offered.

George started straightening up while Nancy and Bess went to get the cleaning supplies. Bess grabbed a rag for dusting. Then she helped Nancy drag the vacuum cleaner to the living room. When Nancy turned it on, Chip raced out of the room.

"Girls?" Hannah called from upstairs. "What's going on down there?"

"We're just helping out," Nancy shouted back cheerfully over the roar of the vacuum.

"Wait until Hannah sees what a good job we're doing," Nancy said to Bess and George. "She'll never want to leave!"

"Hey, Nancy," George called. "I found this under the couch." She held up a shiny gold pen.

Nancy glanced up. "That's my dad's favorite pen," she said. "He was looking for it before he left on his trip. We should put it back in his study."

"I'll do it," Bess offered.

"Okay, catch!" George tossed the pen to Bess.

Bess reached out to catch it, but missed. The pen bounced off her fingertips—right into Nancy's path. Before Nancy realized what had happened, the vacuum had sucked the pen right up.

She switched off the machine as quickly as she could, but it was too late.

"I'm sorry," Bess cried.

"No, I'm sorry," George said. "I shouldn't have thrown it."

"Don't worry," Nancy said. She unplugged the vacuum and opened the front panel. "All we have to do is dig the pen out of the bag."

Nancy tugged at the mushy paper sack inside the machine, but it didn't budge. "It's stuck," she said.

"Let me try," George said. She yanked at the bag, hard. It came loose with a jerk and ripped open. A cloud of gray dust filled the air as clumps of dirt flew out of the bag. One of them landed on Bess's arm.

"Eeewww!" Bess flicked it off, and the clump exploded in midair. "Aaah, aaah." She put her finger underneath her nose. "Phew," Bess said. "I thought I was going to sneeze."

George laughed. "You have gray hair, Bess."

"So do y—aaah, aaah . . ." Bess grabbed her cousin's arm.

"We look like Old Crabapple!" Nancy added. "Gross!"

Bess sighed. "My sneeze went away again," she said, and shook the dust from her hair.

"ACHOOOOOOOOO!"

The three friends burst out laughing.

Nancy reached into the vacuum bag up to her elbow to get her father's pen. When she pulled it out, more dirt spilled onto the rug. Nancy's arm was fuzzy and gray.

At that moment Hannah appeared in the doorway, carrying a suitcase. When she saw the mess the girls had made, she let out a gasp and dropped the suitcase on the floor.

"What on earth is going on here?"

Nancy looked at Hannah's angry face. Uh-oh, she thought. We're in *big* trouble!

5

Flower Power

We were just trying to help," Nancy said in a small voice. "We found Daddy's pen."

But Hannah wasn't listening. She was busy looking at the dusty gray carpet, the yucky rag lying on a table, and the girls' dirty faces.

"We're sorry," Bess said. "We'll clean it all up."

Hannah sighed. "Don't worry, girls," she said. She picked up the suitcase, but it snapped open, dumping a pile of clothes on the floor.

Nancy, Bess, and George ran over to pick them up.

"I'll take care of it," Hannah said quickly. "Why don't you go outside and play?"

"But we want to help clean up," Nancy insisted, handing Hannah a long red dress.

"Wow, I bet you look great in that, Hannah," George said, looking at the gown.

"I used to," Hannah said. "But I'm afraid this one doesn't fit me anymore." She glanced at the pile of clothes on the floor. "Most of these don't."

Hannah started to pick up the rest of the clothes. "Go along now," she said to the girls. "I'll get this done more quickly on my own."

Nancy, Bess, and George washed up, then went out to the yard. Chip followed the girls outside and started sniffing around near the house.

"We really messed up, huh?" Bess said.

"That's not the worst part," Nancy

said. "You both saw the suitcase. Hannah's packing already. That's another clue that shows we're right about her secret. She must be sure she's getting the job at Old Crabapple's.

"First there was the note and the phone call to Joan," Nancy continued. "Then we found out she was meeting with Old Crabapple, who needs a housekeeper. Now this."

"Hey," George said suddenly. "Is Chip supposed to be digging there?"

Nancy saw Chip wagging her tail and growling as she made a hole under a red-leafed bush near the house. Nancy ran over to pull the playful puppy away.

"Stop it, Chip!" Nancy scolded. "Hannah's already mad at us. She'll probably throw you in doggie jail if you mess up the plants in the yard, too."

Then Nancy stopped talking. "I've got it!" she cried after a moment. "Hannah loves gardening. And Chip and I ruined her favorite houseplant last week. It was just about to bloom. Why don't we get her a new one with pretty flowers?"

"That's a great idea," Bess said. "Then maybe she won't be so mad."

"Where can we get one?" George asked.

Nancy looked at her watch. They still had more than an hour until Bess and George had to go home for dinner. "We'll ask Hannah if we can go for a walk," Nancy said. "Then we'll go to Pete's Garden Center. It's only a few blocks away. All we need is some money."

Nancy took Chip inside and got her piggy bank, while Bess and George checked their pockets. When they counted up their money all together, they had enough to buy at least one nice plant for Hannah.

When they arrived at the garden center, they found the owner, Pete, watering some trees.

"Hi," Nancy said. "We'd like to buy a houseplant."

"One with flowers, please," George added.

Pete scratched his chin thoughtfully. "None of my houseplants are blooming right now," he said. "I've got some with colorful leaves, though. How about that?"

Nancy shook her head. "Nope. We need one with flowers. It's very important."

Then she had another idea. If Nancy bought Hannah some pretty flowers for the yard, she might remember her promise to teach Nancy about gardening. Maybe then she wouldn't want to leave.

"It's a little late in the year for outdoor flowers," Pete said. "Are you sure you don't want some bulbs instead? If you plant them now, they'll be beautiful in the spring." He pointed to a picture of some colorful tulips. Below it was a bin full of dirty brown things that looked like dried-up onions.

Nancy wrinkled her nose. "No, thank you," she said.

"Okay," Pete said. He led them outside and pointed to a row of colorful potted flowers. "These are asters," he said. "They'll be blooming for a while."

Bess hurried forward as Pete went back inside. "Ooh, look at the colors."

"I like the purple ones," George said.

"Me, too," Nancy said. "But the blue ones are pretty, too. I think we have enough money to get one of each."

Bess shook her head. "We should get the pink ones," she said firmly. "They look the most cheerful."

Just then Nancy heard a voice behind her.

"What are *you* doing here?"

Nancy turned and saw Brenda standing with her mother. "Um, we're just looking around," she said.

"Really?" Brenda said.

Nancy could tell Brenda didn't believe her.

Luckily George came to the rescue. "We're here picking up some stuff for my mom," she said coolly, and grabbed two pots of pink asters.

"Bye, Brenda," Bess said with a smile.

The three friends went back into the store.

Nancy looked back at Brenda. She was watching her with narrowed eyes. Nancy was glad Brenda was with her mother and couldn't follow them.

The girls had just enough money for the two pots of asters. They carried the plants back to Nancy's house.

"Where should we put them?" Nancy asked.

"Over there," Bess said. She pointed to a square of dirt right under the kitchen window.

"Perfect," Nancy said. She carefully dumped the plants out of their pots.

Then the girls dug two holes in the soft dirt with their hands.

"What's this?" George asked. She grabbed something out of the hole. "Hannah must have planted onions."

Nancy didn't look up. "Put it in the grass," she said. "We'll give it to her later." Then she picked up a plant and placed it in the hole. While she held it straight, Bess and George gently patted the earth down around it.

Within minutes, the second plant was in place. "Awesome," Bess said, clapping her hands. "I told you pink was the best color."

"I can't wait until Hannah sees them," Nancy said.

Just then the girls heard the kitchen window open above them, and Hannah's voice rang out.

"Oh, no!" she cried. "Stop!"

6

All Washed Up

Nancy looked down at her dirty jeans. Was that why Hannah was so upset?

But Hannah's next words explained everything. "My bulbs!" she cried. "Don't move—I'll be right out."

"George, where did you throw that onion?" Nancy asked. "We need it, quick."

"It's somewhere over there." George pointed to where she had tossed it. "Why?"

"I think you might have dug up a bulb," Nancy said, remembering the bin at Pete's Garden Center. "We have to find it before Hannah comes out."

The girls scrambled to search for it.

"I found it," Bess said, and handed the bulb to Nancy.

Nancy looked at it. She was right. The bulb looked just like the ones she had seen earlier.

Hannah came out the back door and hurried over. "Why are you pulling out my tulips?" she demanded angrily.

Nancy's eyes filled with tears. "We wanted to make you a garden. We didn't know you'd planted tulips."

"Oh," Hannah said. She didn't look so angry anymore. She put her arm around Nancy. "What a nice thought," she said. "I'm sorry for yelling. It's just that I spent all morning planting tulip bulbs in this flower bed."

"I'm sorry we ruined them," Nancy said.

Bess and George apologized, too.

"You didn't," Hannah assured them. She looked at the plants and smiled. "Pink is my favorite color."

"But what about your bulbs?"

Nancy asked. She handed Hannah the one George had dug up.

Hannah knelt down and used her hands to make a small hole in the earth near the new plants. She stuck the bulb in with the pointed end up, then pushed some dirt into the hole.

"There," she said. "No harm done. Now we can enjoy your lovely flowers all autumn, and in spring my tulips will come up around them."

"Do you think Daddy will like the flowers?" Nancy asked.

"Of course," Hannah said, looking down at them. "By the way, Nancy, your dad called today. His business is taking longer than he thought, so he won't be home until tomorrow afternoon. I have an important appointment, so I've arranged for you to spend the morning at George's house. Okay?"

Nancy nodded, giving her friends a worried glance. They all knew where Hannah was going on Saturday.

"It's almost dinnertime," Hannah said to Bess and George. "I'm sure your families are expecting you. And, Nancy, you'd better change out of those dirty clothes. Just leave them by the washer."

"Okay," Nancy said. "I just want to say goodbye to George and Bess first."

As soon as Hannah had gone inside, Nancy whispered, "We've got to do something—and fast."

George nodded. "But what? Hannah's interview is tomorrow."

"I know!" Bess cried. "Let's make her a superspecial breakfast before she leaves."

"Great idea," Nancy said. "Can you guys come over early to help?"

"We'll be here," George promised, crossing her heart.

Bess did the same.

Early the next morning, while waiting for Bess and George to arrive, Nancy had another idea. Hannah hadn't had a chance to do the laundry the evening before. Nancy's dirty clothes were still sitting beside the washing machine. She loaded in her jeans and T-shirt. But the washing machine still looked almost empty.

Just then Nancy heard a knock at the door and hurried to let in Bess and George. "Hannah hasn't come downstairs yet," she said. "I think she's still in the shower."

"Good," Bess said. "Then we have plenty of time to get breakfast ready."

Nancy nodded. "Right. But I have something else for us to do first." She told her friends her plan to give Hannah an extra surprise by doing the laundry.

The three of them tiptoed around the house, looking for more clothes to fill up the washing machine. They put in the sheets and pillowcases from Nancy's bed, several of her father's shirts, the rug from the downstairs bathroom, and the towel from Chip's doghouse.

"That should do it," Nancy said, tossing in her favorite pair of purple socks.

George read the box of detergent. "It says to put in one and a half scoops of soap."

"And more if the clothes are really dirty," Bess added.

Nancy looked inside the machine. "This stuff is really, *really* dirty," she said. "I think we should put in the rest of the box."

"Okay." George poured the detergent into the washing machine.

Nancy turned it on.

Then the girls went out to the kitchen and got to work. George squeezed oranges for juice. Nancy made toast with honey, just the way Hannah liked it. Bess set the table.

"What's this?" Hannah asked when she came into the kitchen a few min-

utes later. She was wearing her rose-colored suit.

"Surprise!" the girls cried.

"We made you breakfast," Nancy explained.

Hannah smiled. "I didn't forget my own birthday, did I?"

"Nope," Nancy said. "We just felt like doing it."

"You have been *very* helpful lately," Hannah said, sitting down at the kitchen table.

The girls watched as Hannah ate her toast and drank her juice. "That was delicious," Hannah said when she had finished. "Thank you, girls."

Nancy took Hannah's empty plate to the sink. "We'll wash up."

Just as Nancy was about to turn on the water, she heard a very strange sound:

Thump! Clump! Clank!

7

Spying On Hannah

The laundry!" Nancy cried. She ran to check the machine. Bess, George, and Hannah were right behind her.

The washing machine was shaking so hard it looked as if there were a monster inside. They all watched in horror as a thick foam of bubbles poured out from under the lid.

Hannah stepped forward, being careful not to slip on the wet floor. She switched off the machine, and the noise stopped. So did the bubbles.

Hannah peered into the machine and groaned. She turned around and looked at Nancy, her hands on her hips.

"You know better than to touch the washing machine when I'm not around, Nancy," Hannah said sternly. She looked at the mess on the floor. "You've been nothing but trouble for the past few days. You're father is definitely going to hear about this!"

Nancy looked down at her sneakers. "I'm sorry, Hannah," she whispered.

Hannah looked at her watch and sighed. "I'm going to be late. I'll deal with this when I get back this afternoon."

"Oops," Bess whispered to Nancy as Hannah hurried out of the room.

"Double oops," Nancy whispered back. "I guess we used too much soap."

The girls found Hannah in the hall. "Hurry," she said when she saw them. "Get in the car, and I'll drop you off at George's house."

"That's okay," George said. "Bess and I rode our bikes over here. Can't Nancy ride back with us?"

Hannah thought for a moment. "All right," she said, and quickly called George's mother to let her know the girls were coming. Then they all went outside.

"Goodbye, girls," Hannah said, getting into her car.

Nancy watched sadly as Hannah drove away. "I just wanted to help so Hannah would want to stay. Now I've made so much extra work for her, she's sure to take the job with crabby old Mrs. Garfield."

Nancy, Bess, and George got on their bikes and rode toward George's house.

"I wish we could be there to hear her interview," George said as she pedaled.

Bess nodded. "That way we'd know right away if she got the job or not."

"She'll get it," Nancy said. "Who wouldn't want to hire Hannah?" She paused. "But I guess it couldn't hurt to go over there to try to see what's happening."

When they arrived at George's house, Mrs. Fayne told them they could go for a bike ride. A little while later, the girls were in front of Mrs. Garfield's open gate. Hannah's car was parked in the wide, curving driveway.

Nancy looked at her watch. "It's only ten forty," she said. "Hannah must still be inside. Let's see if we can peek in the window and see her."

"What if we get caught?" Bess asked as they wheeled their bikes through the gates and up the driveway.

"Don't worry," George said. "We won't."

They were almost to the house when they heard the front door open. "They're coming out," Nancy whispered. "Hide!"

The girls ducked behind a row of bushes near the door.

"Thank you so much for meeting

with me," they heard Hannah say. "I can't wait to get started."

"Wonderful," another voice said. "You're just the person I've been looking for to help me."

"That sounds like Old Crabapple," Bess whispered.

Hannah spoke again. "I'll speak to Mr. Drew right away," she said. "I'm sure he'll understand."

"Good," Mrs. Garfield replied. "Then I'll see you a week from Friday."

The front door closed, and a short while later the girls heard Hannah's car drive away.

"This is terrible." Nancy sniffled. "I wish we'd never come here."

"Come on, let's go," Bess whispered. The girls stood up and saw that the big, black gate was slowly swinging shut.

"Hurry!" George cried. "Or we'll be trapped!"

The friends leaped onto their bikes

and rode as fast as they could. They made it through the big gate just as it clanged shut behind them.

"That was close," Bess said, her voice sounding shaky.

Nancy nodded. "We're lucky Old Crabapple didn't see us."

The girls slowly rode their bikes back to George's house.

Nancy was very quiet. Usually she loved solving mysteries. But solving this one was no fun at all. The solution meant Hannah was leaving.

Nancy was thinking so hard that she almost didn't see Brenda sitting on her bike at the end of George's driveway.

"Ugh," George whispered. "What's Miss Nosy doing here?"

"Hi, George," Brenda called with a smirk. "Where are your mom's new flowers? I came over to see them, but I can't find them anywhere in your yard."

Nancy gave her friends a worried

look. If Brenda found out they had lied yesterday, she'd never give up.

George looked worried, too, but Bess smiled sweetly at Brenda. "The flowers aren't here," she said.

Nancy gasped. What was Bess doing?

"They're at Nancy's house," Bess went on. "We didn't tell you yesterday because they're a welcome-home gift for Mr. Drew. We didn't want you to blab about it and spoil the surprise."

Brenda didn't even seem to notice the insult. "That's not a big secret," she said, disappointed. "Who wants to write about that?" Then she pedaled away.

"Good one, Bess." Nancy grinned and gave her friend a hug. "I was afraid she was going to snoop around until she found out about the *real* mystery."

Her smile faded as she remembered what they had just heard at Mrs. Garfield's house.

When Nancy and her friends went inside, Bess's mother was having tea at the kitchen table with her sister, Mrs. Fayne. The girls said hello and went upstairs to George's room.

"This can't be happening," Nancy said, throwing herself on George's bed.

"We can't let it happen," George said. "There's still got to be a way to change Hannah's mind."

Bess shrugged. "How? You heard her. She wants to start a week from Friday."

"I still don't understand why she wants to leave," George said.

Nancy rolled onto her back. "Old Crabapple probably offered her tons of money."

"Maybe you can convince your dad to pay Hannah more," Bess suggested.

"Maybe. I'll see if he's home yet." Nancy ran downstairs and called her house. But nobody answered.

By lunchtime the girls still hadn't

come up with another plan to get Hannah to stay. They ate their peanut butter and jelly sandwiches quietly. At the same time, Mrs. Fayne and Mrs. Marvin talked about the charity auction their volunteer group was holding.

After lunch Nancy called home again. This time her father answered.

"Daddy!" she cried, glad to hear his voice. "Can I come home now?"

"Sure, Pumpkin," he said. "I can't wait to see you."

Nancy said goodbye to her friends and their mothers, and quickly rode off on her bike.

All the way home, she tried to think of the best way to ask her father to give Hannah a raise.

Nancy found him in his study. "Hi there, Pudding Pie," he said, reaching out to give her a hug.

"Hi, Daddy," she said, squeezing him back. "How was your trip?"

"Just fine," he said. "Did I miss anything exciting around here?"

"Not really." Nancy tried to sound casual. "But I was thinking, isn't it time to give Hannah more money? I mean, she works so hard. She deserves it."

Mr. Drew raised an eyebrow. "I agree, Nancy," he said. "That's why I gave her a raise just a couple of months ago. Why are you so concerned about Hannah's salary all of a sudden?"

Nancy bit her lip. She couldn't keep a secret from her father. "I think Hannah found another job," she blurted out. "Hannah's going to leave!"

"What?" Mr. Drew looked surprised. "Why do you think that?"

Nancy began telling him about her clues. When she started to describe Hannah's suitcase, she paused and thought for a second. "Wait a minute," she said slowly. "I just remembered something. Most of the clothes in that suitcase didn't fit Hannah. She said so herself. Why would she be taking them?"

"Hmm. Go on," her father said.

Nancy told him about the conversation she had overheard at Mrs. Garfield's house that morning.

"It certainly sounds as if you might be right," Mr. Drew said. "But do you have any solid proof?"

Nancy thought about it. Before she could answer her father, the doorbell rang. "I'll get it." She ran to open the door.

When Nancy saw who was there, she forgot about everything.

Old Crabapple was standing right in front of her!

8

Hannah's Real Secret

What are *you* doing here?" Nancy asked.

Mrs. Garfield looked startled. "I beg your pardon, young lady." Her voice was very stern.

Up close, Nancy thought that Mrs. Garfield's face looked more like a wrinkled-up crabapple than ever. "I'm looking for Hannah Gruen. Is this the right house?"

"You can't take her yet!" Nancy shouted.

"Take her?" Mrs. Garfield said. "What do you mean? I'm here to return this. She left it at my house."

Mrs. Garfield held up Hannah's address book.

"Who is it, Nancy?" Mr. Drew said. Nancy's father had walked up behind her.

Mrs. Garfield introduced herself.

Mr. Drew shook her hand. "Nice to meet you, Mrs. Garfield," he said. "Hannah has told me such wonderful things about the work you've done for the community."

Nancy frowned. Her father knew who Old Crabapple was. What did that mean? And what community work was he talking about?

"Good," Mrs. Garfield said with a smile. "I hope that means you'll let me steal Hannah away from you for a couple of days. She's just the right person to help me with my next event."

A couple of days? Her next event? Suddenly Nancy realized what Mrs. Garfield was talking about—and what Hannah's *real* secret was.

She waited until Mrs. Garfield said goodbye and had walked back to her car. Then Nancy turned to her father. "Daddy, you knew the real answer all along."

Mr. Drew laughed as he shut the door. "I guess that means you've finally figured it out."

Nancy followed her father into the living room and sat beside him on the couch. "Hannah's helping Old Crab— I mean, Mrs. Garfield, with her charity, right? That's what the meeting was about. And that's what the old clothes and stuff in the suitcase were for. Hannah's giving them away."

Her father nodded. "You solved it, Pudding Pie."

Nancy looked at her father. "But why didn't you tell me right away?"

Mr. Drew ruffled her hair. "I wanted to hear your clues first."

"They all seemed to make sense," Nancy said. "But I guess I was looking at them the wrong way."

Just then they heard the front door open. A moment later Hannah came into the room. Nancy leaped up and ran to give her a hug. "I'm sorry about the laundry this morning," she said.

Hannah hugged her back. "I'm sorry I yelled at you. But why are you and your friends so eager to help out these days? You're running me ragged."

"I thought you were going to take another job and leave us," Nancy said. "I thought if I showed how much help I could be, you would stay."

Hannah looked at Nancy and Mr. Drew. "Leave?" she exclaimed. "What made you think such a thing?"

Nancy explained her clues. "You don't usually wear a suit," she said. "And people wear them when they're looking for jobs. Bess's mom said Mrs. Garfield needed a new housekeeper." She blushed as she remembered spying on Hannah. "And I kind of overheard you talking to Joan on the phone. You told her Mrs. Garfield was a great boss."

"Yes, I did," Hannah said. "That's because I wanted to recommend Joan for the housekeeper's job, since the family she works for is moving to Florida."

"It *was* quite a coincidence that Mrs. Garfield needed a new housekeeper at the same time Hannah was meeting with her," Mr. Drew said. "That's the trouble with circumstantial evidence. It often leads to the wrong answer."

"Circumstantial?" Nancy repeated.

Her father smiled. "That means evidence that seems to support your answer, even though it doesn't really prove it."

Nancy nodded. She was going to write down the word in her notebook later.

"I'm glad the circumstantial evidence was wrong," she said. "I was so scared Hannah was going to leave.

That's why I tried to do all that stuff to help—even though I mostly just ended up making a mess." She told her father about all the things she had done.

He laughed when he heard about the laundry disaster. "I made the same mistake myself the first time I used that machine," he said. "And to help Hannah out, why don't you and I take care of it after dinner?"

Nancy looked at Hannah. "And maybe next spring I could help you plant more flowers in the backyard," she said hopefully. "That way you'll really have a reason to stay forever."

Hannah hugged her. "All the reason I need is here in this room. You're like a family to me—no circumstantial evidence will ever change that."

That made Nancy feel much better. "There's still one clue I can't figure out," she said. "Why didn't you let me into your room the other night?"

Hannah was quiet for a second.

Then she grinned. "I guess you caught me," she said at last. She hurried out of the room while Nancy and her father exchanged a puzzled look.

A moment later Hannah returned. She was holding a pretty notebook covered with flowered cloth and decorated with ribbons. "Here," Hannah said, handing it to Nancy. "I should have known better than to try to surprise such a good detective."

Nancy opened the book. On the first page, in Hannah's neat handwriting, was the recipe for apple cake.

"I'm going to write down all the recipes I teach you," Hannah said. "That way you'll have them all in one place when you're ready to cook on your own—someday far, far in the future, that is," she added with a grin. "After all, you're not allowed to use the oven until you're at least ten."

Nancy gave Hannah another big hug.

*　　　*　　　*

That night before she went to sleep, Nancy took out her notebook. She opened it to her latest mystery and began to write:

I'm glad nosy Brenda never found out about *this* mystery! I can't believe I was so wrong about everything. But I'm glad I was. I should have known that Hannah would never leave just to get a raise or live in a big house. That's not how things work in a family.
Case closed.

TAKE A RIDE
WITH THE KIDS ON BUS FIVE!

Natalie Adams and James Penny have just started
third grade. They like their teacher, and they like
Maple Street School. The only trouble is, they have
to ride bad old Bus Five to get there!

#1 THE BAD NEWS BULLY
Can Natalie and James stop the bully on Bus Five?

#2 WILD MAN AT THE WHEEL
When Mr. Balter calls in sick,
the kids get some strange new drivers.

#3 FINDERS KEEPERS
The kids on Bus Five keep losing things.
Is there a thief on board?

#4 I SURVIVED ON BUS FIVE
Bad luck turns into big fun
when Bus Five breaks down in a rainstorm.

BY MARCIA LEONARD
ILLUSTRATED BY JULIE DURRELL

 A MINSTREL® BOOK

Published by Pocket Books

1237-04

FULL HOUSE™
Michelle

A MINSTREL® BOOK
Published by Pocket Books

Simon & Schuster Mail Order Dept. BWB
200 Old Tappan Rd., Old Tappan, N.J. 07675

Please send me the books I have checked above. I am enclosing $_____ (please add $0.75 to cover the postage and handling for each order. Please add appropriate sales tax). Send check or money order--no cash or C.O.D.'s please. Allow up to six weeks for delivery. For purchase over $10.00 you may use VISA: card number, expiration date and customer signature must be included.

Name _____

Address _____

City _____ State/Zip _____

VISA Card # _____ Exp.Date _____

Signature _____

1033-20

THE NANCY DREW NOTEBOOKS®

by Carolyn Keene
Illustrated by Anthony Accardo

Simon & Schuster Mail Order Dept. BWB
200 Old Tappan Rd., Old Tappan, N.J. 07675

A MINSTREL BOOK
Published by Pocket Books

Please send me the books I have checked above. I am enclosing $_____(please add $0.75 to cover the
postage and handling for each order. Please add appropriate sales tax). Send check or money order--no cash
or C.O.D.'s please. Allow up to six weeks for delivery. For purchase over $10.00 you may use VISA: card
number, expiration date and customer signature must be included.

Name _____
Address _____
City _____ State/Zip _____
VISA Card # _____ Exp.Date _____
Signature _____ 1045-14